The Addicted Collection

Books 1, 2 & 3

By **Faith N. Love**

© Copyright 2019 by The Door 2 Success Publishing All rights reserved.

This document is geared towards providing exact and reliable information in regards to the topic and issue covered.

The publication is sold with the idea that the publisher is not required to render accounting, officially permitted, or otherwise, qualified services. If advice is necessary, legal or professional, a practiced individual in the profession should be ordered.

From a Declaration of Principles which was accepted and approved equally by a Committee of the American Bar Association and a Committee of Publishers and Associations.

In no way is it legal to reproduce, duplicate, or transmit any part of this document in either electronic means or in printed format. Recording of this publication is strictly prohibited and any storage of this document is not allowed unless with written permission from the publisher. All rights reserved.

The information provided herein is stated to be truthful and consistent, in that any liability, in terms of inattention or otherwise, by any usage or abuse of any policies, processes, or directions contained within is the solitary and utter responsibility of the recipient reader. Under no circumstances will any legal responsibility or blame be held against the publisher for any reparation, damages, or monetary loss due to the information herein, either directly or indirectly.

Respective authors own all copyrights not held by the publisher.

The information herein is offered for informational purposes solely, and is universal as so. The presentation of the information is without contract or any type of guarantee assurance.

The trademarks that are used are without any consent, and the publication of the trademark is without permission or backing by the trademark owner. All trademarks and brands within this book are for clarifying purposes only and are the owned by the owners themselves, not affiliated with this document.

A Note To The Reader

First and foremost **THANK YOU** for purchasing my books. I am grateful for every purchase that is made because I get to live my dream of being a writer.

What makes it even more fulfilling is your feedback. **PLEASE** leave me A REVIEW from the source you purchased the book. Tell me what you liked or disliked so that I can continue growing as a writer.

ALSO, check out the **OTHER BOOKS** I have to offer.

https://www.amazon.com/Faith-N.-Love/e/B016U0ZRCO

I would love to get to know my readers so that I can write what you want to read and also to create friendships with people all over the world. So **THANK YOU** for your purchase and support and I look forward to hearing from you.

Table Of Contents

BOOK #1

Mr. Perfect 8

BY FAITH N. LOVE 8

The Addicted To Love Collection Vol. #1 8

Book #1 8

MR PERFECT 10

DINNER 20

THE POOL SCENE 26

LUNCH 35

THE CLIMAX 53

In Love 74

With The Call Girl 74

Book #2 74

HER!! 75

Meeting Ana 81

Burning Desire 91

Jealousy 105

The Wife 110

A New Beginning 116

I'm In Love With My 121

Best Friends Man 121

Book#3 121

Temptation 122

The Bahamas 132

The Moment 139

Back Home 145

The Lie 152

A Preview Of 156

The Naughty Secrets 156

Of A Sex Addict 156

The Forbidden Fantasies Collection Secret #2 156

Mr. Perfect
BY FAITH N. LOVE

The Addicted To Love Collection Vol. #1

Book #1

By Faith N. Love

Disclaimer:
This book contains <u>very hot</u> and <u>explicit</u> descriptions of <u>romantic activity</u>.

Only **mature** readers should read this book.

MR PERFECT

"Please go ahead and screw his brains out, just don't go falling in love with each other."

Avoiding choking on her coffee, Tracy blinked and tried to figure out what Laura had really said, because she certainly hadn't just suggested that Tracy have sex with her costar, who happened to be Laura's flawless husband, Marco Dayne.

However, the next few words out of Laura's mouth, seemed to confirm this impossibility. Laura just took another sip of her coffee and began to elaborate, "I'm his wife.

It's not like I am not going to notice these things. Besides, nothing spices up our sex life like a little affair. If you want to think of it as doing me a favor, go ahead."

Tracy swallowed and laughed nervously. She would be lying if she said that she hadn't noticed the fact that Marco was absolutely gorgeous, long before this moment.

Dayne looked like a perfect ken doll. His metaphorical sculptor had gone overboard. She wasn't planning on making any moves on Dayne, despite his incredible attractiveness.

Besides, he was married to her good friend Laura. Tracy looked laughingly at Laura "Not to mock your generous offer but my boyfriend James isn't exactly the sharing type"

This was a trap that she was determined not to fall into. She wasn't the home wrecker type.

Laura and Dayne had a lovely life, lovely kids and she was not the kind of person to interfere with that, even if the mans wife was trying to trick her into trying it.

Sure, sometimes when he was acting lovesick over her character it was easy to imagine any number of unprofessional interactions.

Acting was like that. It didn't mean anything. She loved her boyfriend. James kept her sane when the crazy soap opera industry she had chosen threatened to relieve her of her good sense.

With him she felt safe and free and she knew who she was and where she stood. Laura smiled slyly and sipped at her drink.

Tracy had to admit, Laura had found a weakness, though she wasn't sure how.

The truth of the matter was that she did think about it, and that there was probably no excuse for thinking about another man, at home in bed with the man she loved.

It wasn't all the time but it did occasionally happen and it would feel awkward when she remembered it at work the next day.

She could say she was just considering how her tv character Diandra felt or could feel about Dayne's character Matt.

In case anyone was wondering. If he ever actually made a move Diandra would be totally into it.

Thinking about how his breath tickled her neck made her shiver and consider what his mouth would feel like against her collarbone.

She'd gotten better at drawing lines between acting and reality over the years. Turning the character and their feelings and relationships and experiences on and off was part of being a professional.

Still, any actor who claimed that there was never occasional slippage between character and self was probably a liar. It had gotten iffy at some points with Jeremy, who wasn't gorgeous like Dayne in the least.

What Jeremy was is a ridiculous flirt and a bit of a bad boy. Nonetheless, there had even been a few times in her trailer where some lines had been crossed.

Neither Dayne nor she had ever even approached this, they were professional and friendly, but Laura must have picked up on their chemistry.

Probably because her husband was ridiculously attractive and it was a safe bet that any woman in his company was sexually objectifying him at any given moment.

Laura dropped the conversation and Tracy was hopeful that she'd passed the test. She wouldn't bring it up with Dayne and hoped that Laura would do the same.

It had to be hard having a husband who would have such an easy time being unfaithful. Hopefully Laura had gotten over this attack of paranoia.

However, Tracy had no idea how committed Laura's was to creating this affair.

DINNER

Less than a week later they went to the Dayne household for dinner. Every time Tracy turned around Laura was refilling her wine glass.

When Laura suggested a trip to the hot tub after dinner, Tracy tried to suggest they head home instead, but was overruled by James' enthusiastic response.

Tracy could have sworn that Laura's obvious smirk was more than her imagination, as she handed Tracy the least covering swimsuit in her collection.

Once they were all settled in the hot water, James initiated the next step of what she knew had started out as Laura's plan.

"It would be so hot to see you kiss him" James insisted, while glancing at Dayne. "What are we, in high school?"

Tracy blurted awkwardly while trying to laugh it off. Tracy was uneasy. This felt like a trap, a test to see if she'd say yes.

"I mean, you kiss people for work without complaining. You could at least put on a show of it, for me." Said Laura while staring into Tracy's eyes

Suddenly Tracy felt insulted, cheapened even. She tried to rationalize that maybe James might have had more than a few or maybe just playing along to be a good sport.

"Marco would be happy to oblige" Laura interrupted, pushing Dayne halfway into Tracy's lap, "Wouldn't you, darling?"

Dayne's expression was an apology, "You are going to frighten off our friends." He told his wife, "Tracy and James didn't sign up for a latchkey party, this isn't the 60s."

"Pretend you are filming this. I never get to see you work." James insisted. Tracy was starting to feel very uncomfortable with this new concept that she was sure he got from Laura.

He pushed her towards Dayne, leaving their noses only a few centimeters away from one another.

"What do you think" Dayne, grinned, trying to diffuse the mood, "Would Diandra make the first move?

Matt certainly doesn't have the nerve to."

"Undoubtedly" she almost whispered.

Laura and James had them almost pinned together and her options were to stare into Dayne's dreamy eyes or look down at his highly toned body.

Just once, she thought, to get them both off her back, to prove to James that it wasn't something she wanted, to prove to them all that it wasn't something any of them wanted.

THE POOL SCENE

She placed her hands on either side of Dayne's face, tilted her head, and leaned in the rest of the way. Her thumbs traced his defined jawbone up to his ears.

Dayne's lips parted against hers and suddenly the kiss became more of a make out than she had planned.

For a moment, she gave in to the enjoyment. This is how Matt would kiss, she had to remind herself. This is how he would respond to Diandra.

This was a scene they were playing out, even if only for a two-person audience. "I think that is about where the scene would cut out."

She commented, as she pulled away at last, trying to emphasize that it was make believe. Unfortunately, James was not letting the idea go.

"More..." he whispered in her ear, having moved in right behind her so that she had nowhere to retreat. He pressed up against her so that she collided with Dayne.

Tracy felt a sickening feeling in her stomach. The aggression, the controlling, it made her feel panicked. She was trapped.

Dayne seemed to notice something in her expression because his attitude went from amused to concerned in an instant.

"I think all this drinking and steam is going to everyone's heads." He interjected, "Maybe it's time we get out.

His arm reached around behind Tracy to hold the edge of the tub in a way that blocked James and gave her room to get her footing.

She was able to push herself up out of the water and get a leg over and onto the solid ground. "Are you serious?" James slurred, "What are you saying she's not good enough for you.

Don't tell me it's your wife; because, I know better." "Relax. I clearly find your girlfriend incredibly attractive.

Why else do you think my eternally generous wife tried to set this whole thing up? It is just obvious that Tracy isn't having fun, that's all.

No insult intended. If you weren't so worried about your pride you would see that she's so tense that she is shaking." Tracy used Dayne's redirection of James' energy as an opportunity to throw clothes on rapidly as she grabbed her purse and phoned a cab.

As Tracy walked away she heard Dayne telling James how lucky he was to have me as a girlfriend.

Then she overheard Dayne telling Laura how he saw Tracy as very attractive and how he knew they would have great sex before Laura jumped in the cab.

By the time that James arrived home, he found the door dead-bolted against him. Tracy silenced his calls and didn't look at the text messages that kept chiming until eventually he gave up.

Tracy wanted to call a friend or her mom, but settled for a cool shower. She had learned long ago that you never complain about your significant other when you are upset about him, the women who love you will never forget or forgive him.

Dayne's words rang in her ears, providing distraction from the despair she felt when thinking about James' behavior tonight. She was pretty sure that Dayne's comments were intended to rile James up, to keep him focused on Dayne so that she could flee.

It was kind. However, Dayne was a good actor, a good storyteller. It had sounded so real, even if she knew better. Just because she was nauseated by James' pushy, voyeuristic, actions didn't mean that she could resist imagining what it would be like to have sex with Dayne.

She wouldn't be able to resist if Dayne really did start at her anklebone and kiss all the way up to her inner thigh and then back down the other leg before slowly sliding her panties down.

She was ridiculously attracted to Dayne, but she was furious at the idea that James tried to push her on another man, like an under booked prostitute.

LUNCH

In the morning, Tracy had seventeen text messages. Most of them were apologies from James, who evidently had sobered up and realized what an ass he had made of himself.

Tracy told herself she should forgive and forget, but alcohol doesn't make you say anything that wasn't somewhere in your mind.

Dayne only left one text message but it was not exactly short. His message was concerned and apologetic.

She ignored all of James' texts for the time being, but briefly replied to Dayne. Telling him not to worry and that she was embarrassed about the night before.

Thankfully, it was a day off from work. By noon an elaborate flower arrangement had arrived via delivery.

James was obviously trying to make amends. Needing something to focus on, Tracy began cleaning out the hall closet.

Halfway through cleaning, Dayne texts her asking if he could bring over lunch. She hesitated for about a minute and a half, embarrassed by his charitable offer, but then accepted.

Looking down at herself, she decided to exchange her sweatpants for denim capris that hit her mid calf and put on a bra under the tank top she was wearing.

She brushed her teeth and washed her face, but didn't put on any makeup to hide the deep circles under her eyes.

She was not trying to seduce anyone, but she wasn't looking for pity either. Dayne showed up with lunch about the time Tracy was on her third cup of tea.

He was wearing a fitted v necked t-shirt and a worn in pair of jeans. The shirt was a grey blue that flattered his skin and brought out his eye color. His hair was perfect as usual.

She probably spent a little too long surveying him before finally, she invited him in.

She proceeded to make more tea as she pulled down dishes and silverware for the food.

Keeping her hands busy kept Tracy from having to figure out what to say. Tracy wasn't sure what aspect of this situation made her the most uncomfortable.

Was it, Dayne's wife's attempts to initiate an affair, her own boyfriend's reaction, last night's kiss, or the fact that she had once again spent time fantasizing about Dayne.

"Not as dramatic of an apology as the flowers." He replied, indicating the arrangement she had left on the counter. "If anyone needs to apologize it isn't you. I still feel so embarrassed."

"Don't be. I am so sorry about last night. Laura means well but she tends to think she knows what's best for everyone.

I told her to leave well enough alone but James isn't a child. No one forced him to act that way."

" Whatever he did or didn't do, you didn't make him do that either. Look, I hope you don't think I was trying to corner you into something."

"Nonsense, I know you were just being nice, like with the food. I know you tried to redirect the situation."

"Because I would never, ever, try and manipulate or pressure you or anyone else into being with me."

"I get that you were just saying those things to keep James' focus on you and let me escape. I appreciate it, really."

"What things?" Dayne looked confused for the first time in the conversation.

Tracy couldn't help but to feel a little embarrassed, "Oh I just mean all of that bit about how you know we would have great sex."

"I meant that. I sort of lost my cool for a minute there and couldn't keep myself from telling your boyfriend how ridiculously lucky he was to have you.

Just because I respect your lack of interest, doesn't mean I stop being aware of how incredibly sexy you are.

I am just sorry if that admission makes this awkward and that my wife's ability to read my attraction put you in an awkward situation."

"You are not just saying that to be nice, right? Because it would be the opposite."

"Cross my heart. I didn't think I was being that subtle." "Tell me again." Dayne stood up and crossed over to stand near Tracy. He took her hands in his and locked eyes with her.

"Tracy Carlyle, you are amazing and hot and I wish that you wanted to sleep with me because I desperately want to sleep with you." "Dayne, you know you are a million times too attractive for it to even be fair."

She replied, standing up so that they were face to face, "I fantasize about exactly that far more often than it is appropriate for me to say." "Appropriate seems increasingly irrelevant."

He breathed, leaning in close. She could feel the heat radiating off of him. She was aware of the way her clothes hugged her body, aware of her own shape.

Her mind raced with images of what might happen next. Then she remembered reality. "Your wife is really as okay with the possibility of our having an affair as she claims to me?" Tracy interrupted, breaking up the moment.

"Amazingly so." Dayne reassured her. "I am honestly not sure how alright I feel with it." Tracy dropped his hands, gathered up the dishes, and walked to the sink and began washing them.

"I mean I want to, but at the same time it seems like the worst idea ever." She put the tea kettle back on the heat and looked anywhere but at Dayne.

In this moment it felt like a great idea to give in to attraction and the ease of his reassurances.

It would serve James right, even. There was a part of her, though, that knew better. It was never that simple.

"What is your worry? I mean what is the worst thing that you think could happen?" Dayne asked.

While leaving the kitchen island between them, rather than invading her space. Dayne was many things, but predatory was not one of them.

After finishing the dishes, she replied finally, "What if I want more or what if you do or what if Laura changes her mind?"

She turned around and looked at him, "What if this is just my way of sabotaging the most serious relationship I have ever had?

What if someone finds out and our reputations are ruined? What if I get knocked up?

What if one of us gets tired of it and not the other and then work is awkward?" Finally she met his gaze as she added, "What if I fall for you?"

Stating her objections only made them more real. "I wish I had all the answers" Dayne sighed. "I have to admit that I don't.

I just know that I want you to the point of distraction and to me it seems worth the risk.

But, it is not just my risk to take, it's yours too. I can't ask you to do what feels wrong to you."

Said Dayne while looking deeply into Tracy's eyes. "I just can't." Tracy told him, with all the strength she had left.

Dayne made a noticeable effort to smile. Tracy watched his handsome face strain as he changed the topic with great deliberation.

She had to open up another box of tea as they chatted away the afternoon, admirably well.

When she walked him to the door, there was an awkward moment as they had to decide how to part. They ended up with cheek kissing and a hug.

Afterwards she closed the door and took another long shower. A long and hot shower was a good time to try and convince herself that it was for the best.

Anyways, she wasn't a romance novel heroine, but she did wish she wasn't alone in the shower.

THE CLIMAX

By the time the water ran cold, she was ready to text James and tell him they would talk when he got home next week.

Of course, she didn't know that the next day was going to be the day on which Dayne literally saved her life.

They were in the middle of shooting and Tracy was trying not to be weird after what had gone on in the last few days.

Somehow it was hard to remember what was a normal amount of eye contact with him.

She must have been looking at Dayne when it happened though; because, she saw the moment his expression went from professional to terrified.

There was no logical reason that her reaction to his crying out her name was to rush towards him, rather than away or to the side.

But that is what she did, just barely missing being crushed by a heavy steel cabinet. She locked eyes with him, her heart pounding as she realized how close she had just come to being crushed.

Adrenaline pumping through her system, she rested her head against his chest and began to shake. He wrapped an arm around her and they walked off set together.

Back in the privacy of her trailer, Tracy wrapped her arms around Dayne's neck and he cradled her face in his hands.

"Are you alright?" His face was full of concern. "Kiss me." She told him. "Are you sure? I mean you've just had a shock." "Kiss me." She repeated, "Yesterday you were willing to take the chances. Today I am."

So he did. She kissed him back. No hesitation, no holding herself back. Each kiss was deep, lingering, and left her breathless. She pressed the length of her body against his.

He brought his hands down along her back, one coming to rest at her hip and the other at her waist. She started unbuttoning his shirt.

They sprang apart abruptly at a knock on the door. It was Brady, coming to check on her. Tracy reassured him that she was fine, just needed a moment to catch her breath.

"They are going to have to recheck all the sets." Brady informed them both, "might as well go home and try and relax." "Come on" Dayne said, "let me escort you home."

Tracy knew he meant more than that by the way he was looking at her. Now that the moment was broken, did she still want to proceed in the direction they bad been headed before Brady's interruption?

She could tell him thanks but no thanks and he would get the message. But she wasn't going to. She was all wound up now and after a near death experience, she couldn't say no to something she actually wanted.

At this point it even seemed like the universe wanted their affair to happen, though she knew that was just her rationalizing. "You'd better" she laughed, trying to seem casual, "Who knows what kind of peril you might need to rescue me from on the way to my apt."

"Maybe a piano falling out a window" Dayne agreed, "or a meteor shower." On the way to her apt, Tracy contemplated how long it had been since she had been with someone new.

She and James had long since settled into a satisfying but somewhat predicable bedroom routine. It had been years since she had to learn the turn on and turn offs of someone new, or even to let someone new know what she liked in bed.

The promise of something new was alluring but slightly nerve-wracking as well. Their first time, like many first times, started out a bit rushed, but that was okay because she was pretty sure that they both knew it was not going to be the last.

They took turns undressing one another, between insistent kisses, as she backed her way into the bedroom and up to the foot of the bed, pulling him along with her. Kicking off her panties from around her ankles.

Tracy laid back on her bed, and dragged Dayne down on top of her. The sensation of his bare skin against her own was exhilarating. Tilting her neck to give him better access as he kissed just above her collarbone, she arched her hips up against him.

Dayne shifted his weight off of her and moved down her body while his hands caressed her ribcage as his lips gently grazed her breasts sending shivers through her body. His pace was somewhat rushed but there was still a gentleness, a butterfly softness to all of his movements.

In someone else it would have been frustrating and made her impatient but in Dayne it was sexy, maybe because it allowed her to romanticize, to forget the wrongness of this encounter and focus on the sweet joy of the moment.

It was hard to think of this as fucking her friend's husband while Dayne made love to her. By the time he got down between her legs, her knees were already weak. He started with her clit, long firm strokes with the flat of his tongue.

She tilted her hips up on instinct, so that his mouth moved lower, tongue against her lips. Dayne moved one hand down, placing his thumb against her clit and leaving the other hand at her hip.

Then with a smooth sweep of his tongue he had her open and ready, as his tongue darted up inside of her, teasing and intensifying the effect of the slow circling of his thumb. The rest of his hand rested against her tingling thigh.

She slid her fingers through his hair. He curled his tongue inside her, making her whole body shake and want more. "Marco..." Her voice came out strange and low, "Please...more." His pace against her clit increased, "Inside." she added, with a press of her hips.

Withdrawing for a moment, he moved his mouth back up to replace his thumb, before slowly sliding his index finger inside her. The pad of his finger hit her sweet spot as he slid it back down against her.

Tracy moaned audibly. Dayne began to establish a rhythm, sliding his other hand over her clit and leaving his mouth free to caress her trembling thighs. She shook more violently and pretty soon all it took was the sensation of a second finger near her entrance to send her over the edge.

Tracy guided him back up her body and enjoyed tasting herself on him as she caught his lips. Still trembling she reached down and guided him inside of her in one swift movement. She could feel his reaction against her lips and her body.

One hand cupped his backside, as the other gripped his shoulder. As he began to thrust, she met each movement with her own, and together they began to build momentum. She ran her hands over his body, enjoying the way he reacted to even her slightest touch.

"Tracy..." he gasped her name, and she renewed their kiss, every inch of her body vibrating and pulsing as she changed the angle of her hips for better access. He moaned into her mouth and as his body began to shake she held him against her, finding her own release a second time.

When he'd recovered his breath a little, Dayne lifted himself off of Tracy, kissing her gently as he collapsed on his back next to her. Tracy wasn't sure what to expect next. As the euphoria faded a little, she wondered whether he was going to get up and leave.

Were things now going to be awkward? Then Dayne reached over and pulled her against him, so that her head rested on his chest in an intimate and comforting pose. Tracy breathed in the scent of sex and the man in bed with her.

She was really going to have to change the sheets she told herself as she drifted off to sleep. When Tracy woke up it was dark and it took her a minute to realize that she hadn't dreamed that sexual encounter up.

She was sort of surprised he had stayed and unsure of what her next move should be. She rolled on her side and looked at the man sleeping next to her.

Sleeping softened her impression of him, but didn't take anything away from his extraordinary good looks.

He looked like some demigod or angel or something, caught sleeping by a mere mortal. Then he opened up his eyes and smiled at her and Tracy found herself kissing him again.

"You are so beautiful." He whispered, pressing their foreheads together. "I'm sure you say that to all the women whose beds you end up in." She tried to joke. "I would hope so.

Otherwise I would be in the wrong bed." He tried to banter back. Then he changed his tone entirely, "Tracy, I hope you don't regret what we are doing here..."

Just hearing him talk about their affair in the present tense was somehow calming, "Hey, not all of us are experts" she told him, "Cut me a little slack for being a novice at elicit affairs. What do we do now?"

"Well it is... not quite ten." he replied, looking at the clock, "I told Laura not to expect me home when we headed over here, so we have until the morning to do whatever we like."

"And what would you like?" She asked. "Well, I believe you overheard me express a couple of the ways I would like to explore your body." He grinned, with a suggestive voice.

"I can think of some exploring I would like to do as well" she whispered into his ear, "But I think my first order of business before that is a shower."

"Am I invited to that shower with you?"

"Required." She promised. Having Dayne in the shower with her was an excellent distraction from thinking about her life choices. His wet body felt heavenly against hers as she pressed him up against the wall of the shower.

There was no question in her mind that there were going to be complications and consequences as a result of the decisions she was making.

Later, she was going to have to deal with the consequences, but in this moment she was going to enjoy running her fingers through his hair, tracing his face with her hands, and watching him squirm as she discovered what spots, on his ridiculously perfect body, were especially sensitive.

The collarbone seemed like as good of a spot to start as any.

THE END

In Love With The Call Girl

Book #2

By Faith N. Love

Disclaimer:
This book contains <u>very hot</u> and <u>explicit</u> descriptions of <u>romantic activity</u>.
Only **mature** readers should read this book.

HER!!

Mike could say that he achieved everything he wanted in life. He was a successful lawyer and he just made partner at his firm.

He was the youngest partner and many of his colleagues envied his him.

His personal life wasn't as successful though. He married his high school sweetheart but as time passed, they grew apart and had very few things in common.

Cynthia, his wife, was a very conservative woman and she often refused to satisfy all of his sexual desires. She was a control freak and preferred to have everything scheduled, including the time and day when they would have sex.

This was usually on Friday nights around 10 pm. They both got used with the life and routines they had.

Just when Mike was beginning to accept the boring reality of his marriage, he saw a young beautiful girl on his way to work.

He always parked his car far away from the office because he loved to walk and this was his only time to get some exercise.

One day, as he was heading to work he saw her again. She was wearing a sexy office outfit and he assumed she was a secretary.

It didn't take long for him to see how wrong he was. A car stopped near her and she bent over to negotiate the price. She was selling her body.

He would have never guessed this by the way she looked. Mike wasn't a judgmental person but seeing her sell her body like this was like a knife to his heart.

He felt that beautiful girl deserved something better. It took a lot of self-control not to go to that driver and kick him in the face.

Her face was beautiful and almost innocent. She was petite with long, black hair. As soon as he laid eyes on her his cock got really hard.

He didn't dare to approach her. He had to protect his reputation and the last thing he wanted was for his wife to find out. The divorce wouldn't be too painful but it would cost him a fortune.

So he walked past her and he went straight to his desk, his hard cock still throbbing in his pants. It has been a while since he had sex and he really need to play with himself.

He called his secretary and asked her to cancel his first meeting. Then he locked the door and dropped off his pants.

Mike imagined her full lips around the tip of his cock. This was enough to make him explode all over his desk.

Meeting Ana

The next day he saw her again. He actually had to wait for her to show up. He couldn't keep on walking without seeing her pretty smile again.

As she passed by him she looked at him and smiled. That smile made him feel butterflies in his stomach.

He knew it was silly. He wasn't a teenager anymore and he couldn't fall in love with a prostitute. She probably just wanted another client.

As he was watching her, he tripped and fell. This was one of the most embarrassing moments of his life.

She tried really hard not to laugh and hurried to his side to help him get up.

"Are you hurt? Let me help you get up."

"Thank you, that's very nice of you. I'm Mike."

"I'm Ana, nice to meet you."

"Let me take you for coffee as a reward for helping me out." He said, not caring anymore if someone saw him with her.

Her captivating big blue eyes made him forget she was a woman of the street. He could have stared in her eyes for hours.

She looked at him with a surprised look. Usually men aren't interested to sit and drink coffee with her.

"I think you know what my job is. I'm still at work now and I can't leave, but if you want to go to a nearby hotel that's another story."

"Well...okay. Meet me at the hotel across the street in 8 hours when I finish my work for the day." He said without even thinking.

"Sure, I will be in room 12."

Obviously that hotel was her place of business. Mike was starting to have regrets but he couldn't help himself. He had to have her even if she needed to get paid for it.

She was like a magnet attracting him and making him forget about his reputation and marriage.

The fact that he had to bring cash made him feel a little weird but it didn't stop him. Mike tried to ignore this little detail.

He told himself that the money would have been spent anyway on an expensive dinner. They were just skipping the meal.

This idea made him feel a little better. He wasn't paying for sex he was just being a gentleman paying for a dinner they weren't going to eat.

That day went by very slow. He kept looking at his watch and he couldn't pay attention during the meetings. All he could think about was Ana.

He couldn't believe that in just a couple of hours he was going to explore that perfect body of hers. His cock was already ready to explode just by thinking about it.

However, that day he didn't touch himself. He already called his wife to let her know that he was working late.

She didn't seem to care too much. She was also going out with her girlfriends.

Cynthia was going out a lot lately but he knew it was because she was feeling lonely at home.

He worked hard to give her the life she wanted but this left him little free time. This is why he had nothing to object when she stayed out late with her friends.

He didn't suspect her of cheating on him because he didn't believe she was that type of woman. She never gave him any sign that she even enjoyed sex.

For her, it was more like something a wife had to do for her husband. At least that was what she let Mike believe.

Little did he know she had her own little secret. Cynthia actually loved having sex, just not with him.

She was actually in love with another man. For her, Mike was just like a bank. She needed him for money because she never worked a day in her life.

Her husband gave her everything she wanted. All she did was shop and visit spa saloons.

Lately she discovered another hobby of having sex with younger men. One of them in particular stole her heart and he was all she could think of.

Burning Desire

As he was walking towards the hotel, Mike could hear his own heartbeat. He couldn't remember the last time he was this nervous and excited.

The receptionist gave him the card key from the room. Ana was already there lying naked on the bed.

Without too many words, she got up and pulled him towards the shower.

She took all of his clothes off and then she started to gently wash every part of his body. She gently caressed on his hard cock, balls and ass hole.

The sensations were getting too much for him. Mike felt that he was about to explode so he asked her to stop.

"I think we are clean enough. I don't want to cum yet."

They moved to the bedroom where she gave him a massage using her own body.

First, she slowly rubbed some nice smelling oil all over her body. Just seeing her massaging her slim body with oil, he could feel his cock pulsing in anticipation.

Then, instead of using her hands for the massage, she used her body. This was something he could only imagine in his hottest dreams.

He thought for a second about his wife. Cynthia would never agree to do this.

Mike then quickly got her off his mind. There was no guilt. He felt that she failed to satisfy him as a woman and wife.

When he entered Ana's surprisingly tight pussy, he lost all control over himself. He needed to ejaculate deep inside.

Her screams of pleasure made him even hotter. He could feel her pussy get wetter every time she had an orgasm.

"Wow...that was..." She tried to speak.

"What is wrong? Wasn't it good? Did I do something wrong?"

"You were amazing. I am not sure if you believe me but usually I don't get turned on with clients. It's all business.

But with you…I just had the most intense orgasm in my life. You know what I am not even going to take your money. Let's just consider this was just for pleasure."

"Are you sure?"

Mike wasn't a cheap man but the fact that she didn't charge him meant a lot to him.

It made him feel like more of a man. He almost felt sorry he couldn't brag about this to anyone.

"Since this isn't business how about we have dinner together?"

"I told my wife that I am going to be late tonight and I would love to get to know you better."

She agreed and they went to the hotel's restaurant. He discovered that she had a very bubbly and fun personality.

As he imagined, she had a serious reason for selling her body. Her mother was really ill and needed money for expensive treatments.

He immediately offered her money but she refused.

"I could never take your money. I prefer to earn them myself. I don't want to take advantage of anyone.

"Don't get me wrong, I hate what I'm doing. I had other dreams for myself…"

"What kind of dreams? What would you like to do?"

"My dream is to work in a big office as an assistant. I have been trying to get a job like that for months but no one is willing to hire me because I have no experience."

When he heard this, Mike couldn't believe his luck. He was looking for an assistant and there she was.

The woman of his dreams was searching for the exact type of job he was offering.

Even if they could never have a real relationship with her, he was happy to make her dream come true.

"Actually, I am looking for a secretary. I am a very successful lawyer. Would you like to work for me?"

Ana jumped off her seat directly into his arms and they started to kiss. She could not express her happiness in words.

This amazing man was giving her the opportunity to start a new life. It was the first time Ana met a man like him.

He was extremely charming, amazing in bed and kind. Other than him being married, Ana had met the perfect man.

Unfortunately, he was married and she knew that this could be their last kiss.

"Don't worry, I know that starting tomorrow you will be just my boss and that nothing can happen between us."

Mike looks at her and while staring in her eyes he says "I really like you and I think I am falling in love with you.

I know it's really fast but I can't deny how I feel. If you don't feel the same way I will understand.

"You are just amazing.

I really like you too but you are married. I am scared that I will end up with my heart broken. I know you would never leave your wife for me."

"The only reason we are still together is because we don't want to split our little fortune."

Later that night they made love again thinking it would be for the last time.

When he got back home, Cynthia was asleep. He was glad he didn't have to give her any explanations.

Ana started her new job early in the morning. She was a smart girl and she didn't need much coaching. It took her less than a week to learn everything.

Jealousy

Mike suspected that he probably wasn't the first client who fell in love with Ana.

She had something special that made men want to protect her and make her theirs. This is why he wasn't surprised when one of them came to look for her at the office.

He kept on sending her flowers and asking her out. Mike knew he had no right to feel jealous but he couldn't help it.

He asked him not to visit the office anymore because it was a place of business.

He couldn't just tell that man to back off because Ana was his. The truth was he was married and a relationship with Ana was impossible.

Mike started to resent his wife. He viewed her as the reason he couldn't be with the woman he loved.

For the first time he could clearly see that all Cynthia cared for was money. They hardly even talked anymore.

He wasn't sure if Ana liked that guy either. He decided to have a serious talk to her.

H called her into his office "Ana, please be honest with me. I know I have no right to even ask you this but I would like to know if you are in love with that guy that keeps on looking for you."

"No of course not, he is just an ex client but I am done with that life now. I am indeed in love but with someone else."

When he heard this, he didn't have courage to ask her who that man was.

She saw the pain in his eyes and said "You silly man, you are the one I love!" and gave him a kiss on the lips.

He locked his office door and bent her over the desk. With one hand he ripped off her panties.

"I would have taken those off." She said with a naughty smile.

He took her hard from behind until they both reached an orgasm at the same time. They knew they couldn't stay apart any longer and from that moment on they were inseparable.

The Wife

Cynthia didn't love her husband anymore. The only reason she was still with him was because she got used to the good life.

She loved to luxurious and expensive things and she knew that she wouldn't be able to afford the same life style if she divorced Mike.

She was having an affair with a younger man but he wasn't nearly as rich as Mike.

She suspected Mike had someone too so she started to follow him. Not out of jealousy, she just wanted proof in case of a divorce.

She wasn't going to let some other woman get her hands on Mike's money. Cynthia hoped it wouldn't get to a divorce.

She waited patiently for a couple of months. When she saw that Mike and Ana were still together, she took matters into her own hands.

She saw no point in arguing with him about his cheating so she decided to go straight to Ana.

She found out where Ana lived and knocked on her door.

She threatened to destroy Mike's career and reputation if she didn't leave him.

She even hired a private investigator who informed her about Ana's past.

She felt like she won the lottery when the investigator told her that Ana used to be a prostitute.

Ana was in shock. She didn't want to destroy Mike's life.

She packed her bags and left town that day without a word to Mike.

When she missed work, Mike tried desperately to reach her. Her phone was off and all her clothes were gone. Mike wasn't himself anymore.

Every day he tried to find her. His wife enjoyed seeing him like this. She felt like she got her revenge and made sure he knew it was her who chased his girlfriend away.

Mike was very angry and heartbroken every time he heard his wife talk bad about the love of his life.

Finally he decided that money and career weren't as important as Ana. Without her, nothing really mattered so he moved out and filed for divorce.

This didn't take long to finalize because they had nothing to share. He gave her everything.

Cynthia couldn't be happier. She was free to enjoy any young man she desired and she didn't have to worry about money. It was like a dream come true.

She decided not to destroy Mike's reputation too. She had taken enough from him.

A New Beginning

It took Mike four months to finally find Ana. When he did, he could clearly see she was pregnant.

He couldn't believe his eyes. It took him a few seconds to recover from the shock.

She was in her new apartment. With one hand she was touching her belly. That baby was the only thing she had left.

She missed Mike deeply and she found comfort in feeling his child growing inside her.

She decided not to look for him because she didn't want to destroy his life.

Ana knew how hard he worked to become a lawyer and partner at the firm.

When he finally found her he looked in her eyes and said "My love, I want to be with you. I left my wife, she got all my money.

I am poor but with a lot of love to offer. I can see you are pregnant and I am willing to be the father of your child no matter who the biological father is."

Ana jumped into his loving arms and said "Well, I am glad, especially since you are the biological father!"

Mike always wanted a child but his wife didn't like kids. He got to a point when he accepted this.

He had given up the hope that he would actually become a father someday. Now all his dreams were coming true.

He had the woman he loved, a baby on the way and luckily he still had his career.

All his wife took was money and he knew he could always earn more.

There was a time when he was obsessed with the superficial life of material things but Ana changed him.

THE END

I'm In Love With My Best Friends Man

Book#3

BY Faith N. Love

Disclaimer:
This book contains <u>very hot</u> and <u>explicit</u> descriptions of <u>romantic activity</u>.
Only **mature** readers should read this book.

Temptation

Alice was happy that her husband finally had some time off work to go to Bahamas for a well-deserved vacation.

They both thought it would be more fun if their friends Stephanie and Karl joined them.

They didn't have any other married friends. The rest were all single and had different lifestyles.

Alice and Mathew had a mortgage to pay and serious jobs. They couldn't afford to spend their nights in clubs like the rest of their friends. This is why this vacation was so important.

She was also hoping to work on her marriage. They were both so focused on their jobs that they forgot how to love each other.

Lately she saw Mathew like one of her friends. They still had fun together but that was about it.

Alice wanted more from her marriage. She wanted that spark they had years ago.

They had no kids yet, so they couldn't use that as an excuse.

Most people who knew Alice thought that she was happiest and luckiest woman in the world. She had a good job and she married her high school sweetheart who seemed to love her more than anything.

However, this was not the case. This was only the impression they gave to the rest of the world. Only the two of them knew what was going on for real in their marriage.

Lately, she felt something was missing from her relationship. Their wedding was just the next logical step they had to take in their relationship.

Both of their parents wanted to see them married and with a lot of babies. So pushed by their families, they decided to get married.

There was no real passion between them. But it wasn't always like this. When they were in high school they would had done anything for each other.

Since then, they both grew up into different people. It was like they were walking on different roads in life.

Mathew was the quiet type. He enjoyed spending his evenings at home with a bottle of beer and a soccer game.

Alice missed the night life in clubs. She envied her single friends who seemed to live life like an adventure.

She missed going out dancing and having men admiring her hot body. She was still a hot woman. She knew this.

Whenever she walked a man of any age, he would turn his head to check her out. She also still received plenty of complements.

Whenever she went out shopping, she took off her ring just to see if she had the same impact on men. She was always happy with the results.

Men would smile and some would approach her to ask for her phone number. This was the only excitement she had left since she was a married woman.

Whenever she was alone and horny, she would play with herself until she reached orgasm. The problem was that with her husband she could never achieve climax.

Alice worried that maybe something was wrong with her body. She even talked to her friend Stephanie about this.

She was very envious when her friend told her how good the sex with her husband was. She wanted that too.

From that day on she saw Stephanie's husband Karl in a new light. He was not just her friend anymore. He was a real man who could please a woman.

Many times she wished that she had married Karl instead of Mathew. These were just dreams that could not hurt anyone. She told this to herself whenever she fantasized about Karl.

When they planned to go together on vacation, she couldn't help but feel excited. That meant she was going to spend a lot of time around Karl.

She had made her peace with the idea of having a life without any passion with her husband.

Alice had no intention of cheating on him but she thought there was nothing wrong with dreaming.

Late one night, when Mathew was fast asleep, she pictured how it would feel if Karl was there instead of him.

In her imagination, he was slowly sucking on her nipples sending shocks of pleasure between her legs. Then she would feel her special spot between her legs getting all wet and she could not stop touching herself.

She would start teasing herself with circular moves around her clitoris. Next, she always put a finger inside.

At that moment, her hips would start rocking. She did that while trying not to wake her sleeping husband next to her.

The thought that any moment he could wake up and see her made her even hotter. It was like she was doing something forbidden and it turned her on.

Whenever Mat turned on the other side, she stopped and held her breath. Alice's heart was beating really fast but she needed to finish what she started.

She felt like she couldn't control the waves of pleasure taking over her. It didn't take more than a few minutes for her to explode in pleasure.

When she was done, she had the impression that she just cheated on Mathew. It was a silly idea but she would have loved to be able to talk to him about anything.

They were good friends and talked about everything but sex. Mathew was a shy man and he did not want to talk about sex.

He never actually asked her if she had an. It was like he didn't believe this was very important to women.

A couple of times she tried to open the subject but without any luck. He would just change the subject.

The Bahamas

It was finally time to go on vacation. When Karl and Stephanie arrived, they all hugged each other as they normally did.

When Alice felt Karl's muscled body pressed to hers she had to take a deep breath. Every time she was around him she acted like a teenager in love.

Before they arrived, she spent hours picking a sexy outfit. For some reason, Alice wanted him to find her attractive.

Even if nothing could ever happen between them, she wanted him to like her more than he liked his own wife. Alice knew she was a lot prettier than her friend, Stephanie.

Sometimes she wondered how a good looking man like Karl even looked at a woman like Stephanie.

She was a little overweight and looked like an ordinary woman. It's not like she didn't like Stephany. Alice considered Stephany her friend.

Lately she was her only friend left since she wasn't so much in touch with the rest.

Alice had no intention in hurting Stephanie. She told herself that a platonic love could not hurt anyone.

At least now she had a man to fantasize about while she was having sex with her husband or whenever she played with herself.

When they got Bahamas, she could feel Karl's eyes on her body. This didn't surprise her at all. The long hours she spent at the gym really paid off.

Stephanie had cellulite and some extra weight. Alice's body was very slim and sexy.

She was happy to see that Karl appreciated this too. She tried to catch him alone even if it was just for a few minutes.

She had her chance when Stephanie and Mathew went to buy something from a grocery store nearby.

She went into his room and they just talked as simple friends.

"Please don't do this," he said.

"What am I doing?" Asked Alice surprised.

"You are biting your lip while you speak and this makes me want to have you right here. It makes me forget that we are both married."

Alice was shocked. She never expected Karl to be so direct. Up until then, there was nothing between them but admiring looks.

They both couldn't deny what they felt for each other. Now there was no way back.

"Karl…this is very inappropriate!" Said Alice trying to sound offended. However, she couldn't remember a moment when she was happier.

This meant he was longing for her body too. If they had more time she would had jumped into his arms right then. However, she was scared that their spouses could be back any minute.

"I know, but I have a feeling you will not get offended by this. I saw you looking at me every time we meet. You want me as much as I want you!"

"Yes, it's true. I am embarrassed to admit it but yes, I am very attracted to you. My relationship with Mathew is not going very well and I need something more in my life.

I would never cheat on him, I hope you know this. What is happening between us is just something platonic."

She didn't believe her own words. She knew that if he insisted she wouldn't be able to refuse him.

However, she also knew that nothing could ever happen between her and Karl. They would have to keep their desire a secret no matter how strong the temptation was.

Karl however, did not agree with this. He spent days looking for the best moment to have sex with Alice.

The Moment

That moment came when both couples where on the beach. Suddenly, Alice said she had a headache and she returned to her hotel room.

"I am going to go too. I am not feeling too well. You two stay, enjoy the sun." He said to Mathew and his wife.

"Must have been something you both ate." Said Stephanie clueless.

He knocked on her door and she opened expecting to see her husband. Her jaw dropped when she saw Karl standing there.

"Where is everyone else?"

"It's just me. We have a couple of hours alone. I couldn't stay away anymore. Your body drives me crazy. I need to have you right now."

"Ow Karl…" She managed to say before he covered her lips with his own.

She couldn't reject him any longer. Alice was burning with desire. He pushed her on the bed and spread her legs.

He was rough but she loved it. Right now it was exactly what she needed. She had no time for romance.

His hands were all over her perfectly round breasts and her belly. He then replaced his fingers with his mouth.

When his tongue got near her wet spot, he moved his head and licked instead the inside of her legs.

Her pussy was burning with desire and she wanted his lips there. He really took his time. He was moving too slow for her.

Karl waited until she actually begged him to lick her between the legs. He did not need to be asked more than once.

His skillful lips and tongue tasted every inch of her wet treasure. He used his tongue to make little circles.

While her hips were moving up and down, with one hand she pushed his head down. For a while there was nobody else in the entire world.

Stephanie and Mathew didn't even exist. She forgot they were nearby on a beach. All she could feel was the intense sensations Karl was bringing to her body.

She never felt this desire and passion with any other man. She reached climax when he slowly sucked her clitoris.

Her body was really trembling and she needed a few seconds to find the strength to move again or stand up. By the time she did this, he was already naked.

His hard penis was practically standing up on its own. He was ready for her. Seeing this made her want him inside her.

She turned with her back towards him and bent over on a table. He understood the invitation and slipped deep inside her.

With one hand he grabbed her hair and then started to move really fast. It was like a wild dance of lust.

It took only a few minutes for her to feel like she was losing control again. It was a feeling she did not want to stop.

However, those waves of intense pleasure were coming again and she gave in. When she reached orgasm again she let out a scream.

A few seconds later he exploded inside her and collapses over her. At that moment she realized they did not use any protection.

Alice did not see the point in using protection since both her and her husband wanted to have kids. She never expected to have an affair.

Back Home

When they got back home, Alice didn't know how things between her and Karl will be.

They started to visit more often and she had the chance to spend more time with him. However, their spouses were always there too.

This didn't leave them any privacy. A couple of weeks passed by like this.

When her period was late she knew she was carrying Karl's child. It has been a while since she last had sex with Mathew so there was no doubt in her mind.

This news made her both happy and unhappy. She was starting to fall in love with Karl. However, she didn't see any way to be with him without hurting two other people.

Also, she wasn't sure of Karl's feelings. The thought that he might leave her kept her up at night.

She called Karl when she knew he was at work and Stephanie was not around. He was happy to hear her voice thinking she was calling for more sex.

They met at a coffee shop and she told him about the baby. This was not good news for him at all. Instead of helping her come up with a good solution, he got up and left.

He also accused her of getting pregnant on purpose. Lately, Karl had realized that all he felt for Alice was physical attraction.

He was still very much in love with his own wife. The affair with Alice made him feel guilty towards Stephanie and this pushed him to be more attentive and a better husband.

In return, Stephanie was a better wife too. They were practically rediscovering each other like in a second honey moon.

He considered Alice helped strengthen his marriage and up until that moment he was grateful for that. When he heard about the baby he realized there was no way he could keep this a secret from his wife.

This meant he was going to lose her.

Separation and Divorce

Karl thought that it was better to hear it from his mouth. He got home and on his knees, he begged for her forgiveness.

Stephanie cried and screamed. He tried to hug her but she pushed him away. She said she could get over the affair but not over the fact that he was having a baby with another woman.

Worst of all, that woman was her friend. She didn't even want to say anything to Alice. She didn't consider she was worth it. Stephanie packed her bags that day and left Karl.

Alice heard all this and she had to confess what happened to her own husband. Unlike Karl, she had no regrets when Mathew left her. There was no more love between them.

All she could think of now was how to get Karl to be with her. She really didn't expect him to realize that he still loved Stephanie. This was a really painful thing to hear from him.

Karl decided that even if his wife never got back with him, he still wouldn't start a relationship with Alice.

He planned to always be in his son's or daughter's life but that was it.

For the next few months Karl tried to get Stephanie back. In the end, she gave in. Stephanie loved her husband very much.

She needed a couple of months to cool off but she understood that if Karl really loved Alice he would have chosen to be with her.

The fact that Alice was now single and Karl was still looking for her, told her enough.

The Lie

Karl was still visiting Alice but it was with his wife's permission. Stephanie knew that there was nothing more important than the baby and he had to be there for Alice.

She trusted him enough not to cheat on her again. She could see how much he regretted it.

All this time, Alice kept on hoping that the pregnancy would make Karl decide to be with her. When she realized this was never going to happen, she told him the truth.

"There is something I need to tell you. Before I tell you, just keep in mind that all I did was out of love for you."

"What happened? What did you do??" He asked worried.

"I was indeed pregnant but I had an early miscarriage a couple of weeks later. I didn't want to tell you because I was hoping you would leave that stupid wife of yours and be with me.

Now that I see this will never happen, I have no choice but to tell you the truth. You would have known soon enough when there was no growing belly and no baby."

When he heard Alice's confession he saw black in front of his eyes. He had never been so angry in his life. That woman played him and played with his marriage and happiness.

He punched the wall to avoid hitting her. That was a big mistake. He hurt himself so bad that he needed to go to the hospital.

"I am coming with you!" She said.

"No, you are not! I never want to see you again in my life!"

Alice was all alone and for a second she wanted to call her husband. She knew that if she begged for his forgiveness he would have come back to her.

However, she learned something from her mistake. She discovered the meaning of real passion and real love.

From now on, she wasn't going to settle for anything less than what she was worth.

THE END

A Preview Of

The Naughty Secrets Of A Sex Addict

The Forbidden Fantasies Collection Secret #2

Serena was getting ready for a very important meeting with a billionaire business man.

She was nervous because she could lose a very big account.

After spending hours in front of the mirror, she was finally ready. This was not at all like her.

Serena was usually very strong and self-confident. It took a lot to make her feel nervous.

"Mister Adam Jones is here." announced her assistant.

"Okay, let him in."

This was the first time they met in real life. She heard a lot about him but no one told her how good looking he was.

His muscles were visible even through the suit jacket. He had green eyes and dark hair.

His smile made her knees buckle and she could already feel that familiar wetness between her legs.

Serena knew it was impossible to go through the meeting without having at least one orgasm. The man standing in front of her was too distracting.

As he was explaining his business plan, she squeezed her knees together. Her hips were slowly moving on the chair.

She was rubbing herself on the chair without even realizing. Luckily, he didn't notice this little detail.

To Purchase The Rest of
Faith N. Love's
Click the book title below:
The Naughty Secrets Of A Sex Addict

The Addicted To Love Collection #1

Printed in Great Britain
by Amazon